$6⁹⁹

 $_⁹⁹

 $3⁵⁰

 $4⁹⁹

 $6⁹⁹

 $2⁹⁹

 $7⁹⁹

 $4⁹⁵

 $6⁹⁹

 $8⁵⁰

 $4⁹⁹

the Underwear Salesman

For Dan Darigan,
noble mon and constant pal
—J. P. L.

Atheneum Books for Young Readers
An imprint of Simon & Schuster Children's Publishing Division
1230 Avenue of the Americas, New York, New York 10020
Text copyright © 2009 by J. Patrick Lewis
Illustrations copyright © 2009 by Serge Bloch
Book design by Sonia Chaghatzbanian
The text for this book is set in Lomba.
The illustrations for this book are digital collage.
Manufactured in China
10 9 8 7 6 5 4 3 2
Library of Congress Cataloging-in-Publication Data TK
ISBN-13: 978-0-689-85325-8
ISBN-10: 0-689-85325-4

the Underwear Salesman

And Other Jobs for Better or Verse

poems by J. Patrick Lewis   illustrations by Serge Bloch

ginee seo books

atheneum books for young readers
new york   london   toronto   sydney

Guess how many jobs there are
At the occupation salad bar!
I've counted fifty-four so far.
So what will you become?

Maybe you have just the flair
For teaching French—*Merci, mon cher*—
Designing brand-name underwear
Or beating the bass drum.

Say, what about a referee,
A truck driver, a maitre d',
A rock star rocking MTV,
A keeper of an inn,

fireman

soldier

A teacher teaching ABCs,
The reigning Mr. Hercules,
A pirate on the Seven Seas . . .
But where do you begin?

If you are unemployed and blue,
And you have nothing else to do,
Then turn the page and maybe you
Can find a job right here!

That's why I wrote this handy guide
(For children overqualified
For boring jobs). Now you decide
Which fabulous career?

chef

Librarian

No one has more fun than I!
I've met Harriet the Spy,
Ferdinand the Bull, and Pooh.
(Eeyore says, "How do you do?")

Mole and Badger, Toad and Rat
Come to dine and stay to chat.
With the Little Prince in hand,
Alice in her Wonderland,

Call of the Wild (a pedig-read),
What else could anybody need?

Fables, folktales, nonsense verse
I carry home in my big purse.
Have as much fun by yourself!
Take a book down from the shelf.

Exterminator

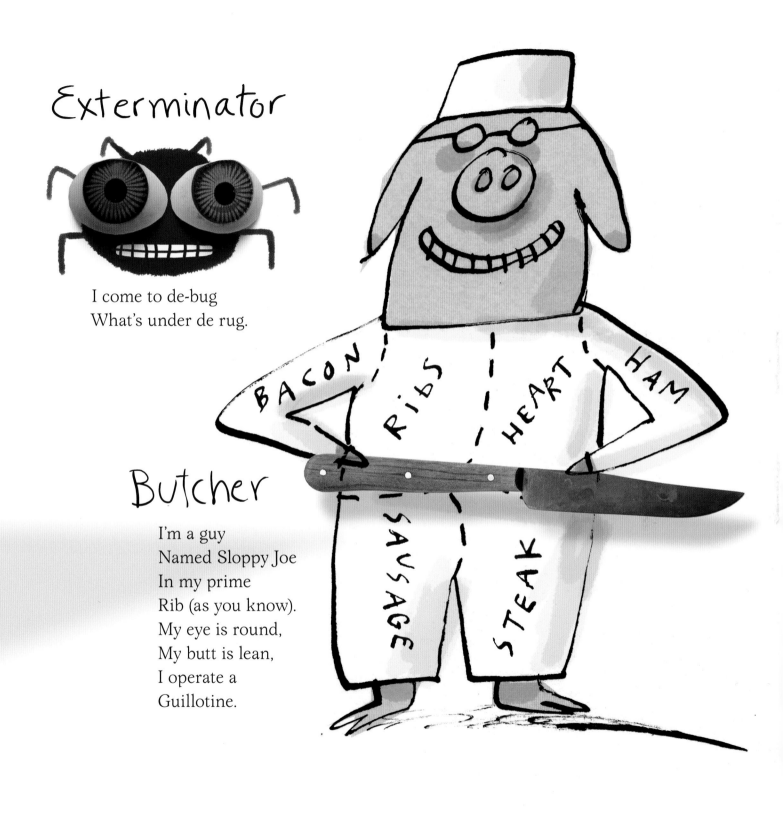

I come to de-bug
What's under de rug.

Butcher

I'm a guy
Named Sloppy Joe
In my prime
Rib (as you know).
My eye is round,
My butt is lean,
I operate a
Guillotine.

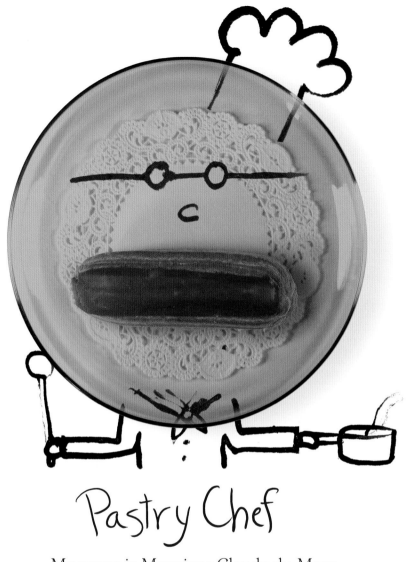

Pastry Chef

My name is Monsieur Claude du Mare.
My specialties—chocolate éclair,
    Cannoli, cream puff 'n'
    Raspberry bran muffin.
But I, Monsieur Claude, shall prepare

My very own recipe for
A delicacy you'll adore—
    Grape jelly on toast!
    Oh, I don't mean to boast,
But the children keep begging for more!

Mapmaker

I climb up a mountain by fine fountain pen.
    I float down a Nile of ink.
I crisscross three countries, six cities, and spend
    A while on an isle to think.

I brush in the valleys and sweep in the sands,
    I shadow blue oceans, green seas.
I'm the very particular painter of lands
    Who measures the world . . . by degrees.

Underwear Salesman

You wear them briefly
      And in short,
I sell them chiefly
      For support.
Whoever met you
      Without a pair
Would not forget you—
      You'd be bare!

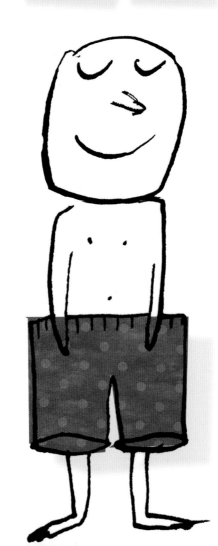

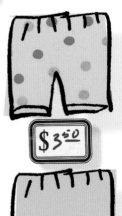

Elevator Operator

Step into my
Rocket room—
Which floor? Eighty-seventh?
Zoooooooooooooom.

"Up?" or "Down?" are words I blurt
All day long. My life is

V

E

R

T.

My next job?
I hope my chore is
On the level, I mean,
H O R I Z.

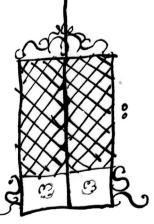

Garbage Collector

Things to do
at work:

· Smash trash
· Squish fish
· Wrap scrap
· Bind rinds
· Close nose

Things to do
after work:

· Hose clothes
· Lose shoes
· Shower (hour)
· Suds crud
· Quench stench
· Comb dome
· Great date

Ice Sculptor

In windchill ten above or five below,
I pour buckets of water in the yard
And watch a monumental ice cube grow,
As people stop along the boulevard
To see a sight they've never seen before.
I take my brush, whisk broom, and chipping blade.
You could pick up at any hardware store
The necessary tools of my trade.
I gaze at this gigantic frozen blob,
Imagining a creature to create.
It's so much fun; it's really not a job.
My motto is ALWAYS REFRIGERATE!

Belly Dancer

Wiggle those hips,
Swivel that torso,
Shake that belly—
Then do it more so!

Acrobat

I tumble twice
Without a hitch,
But if my partner
Gets an itch,
It isn't death-
Defying yet
You mustn't scratch
Without a net!

Poet

I take a word, and then another,
Let them get to know each other,

Exercise them till they learn
A song to sing, a phrase to turn.

I choose strong verbs right off the bat
(Since adjectives are high in fat).

Some words may act excited, nervous,
But all are glad to be of service.

Highway Line Painter

To keep you out of trouble, fellow,
I like to paint lines double yellow.

I usually paint them straight and narrow,
But oh to paint a left-turn arrow!

Auto Mechanic

It wasn't the battery,
Fuel line, plugs,
Rods or distributor,
Bearings or lugs.
The engine ran smoothly.
I thought the next best
Thing to do was to give it
The highway stress test.

I turned the car right,
And it went *clunk-clunk*,
I turned the car left,
And it went *thunk-thunk*.
I swore it was nothing
But a pile of junk
Till I found a bowling
Ball left in the trunk.

Plumber

Here's
A job
To call
Your
Own
When
You're
Inside
The

Twoilet zone.

Dictionary Maker

Nouns are salads,
Verbs are herbs.
I toss adjectives, adverbs

In a feast extraordinary
(Also known as the dictionary).

If you haven't eaten yet,
Try my soup—it's

ALPHABET!

Dog Trainer

Scent of alley cat—
I give my bulldog a quick
Tug-of-warning!

Pet Groomer

A balding, potbellied pig
Came into my shop today.
I made the pig a pixie wig
But she forgot toupee!

CALUMET CITY PUBLIC LIBRARY

Gardener

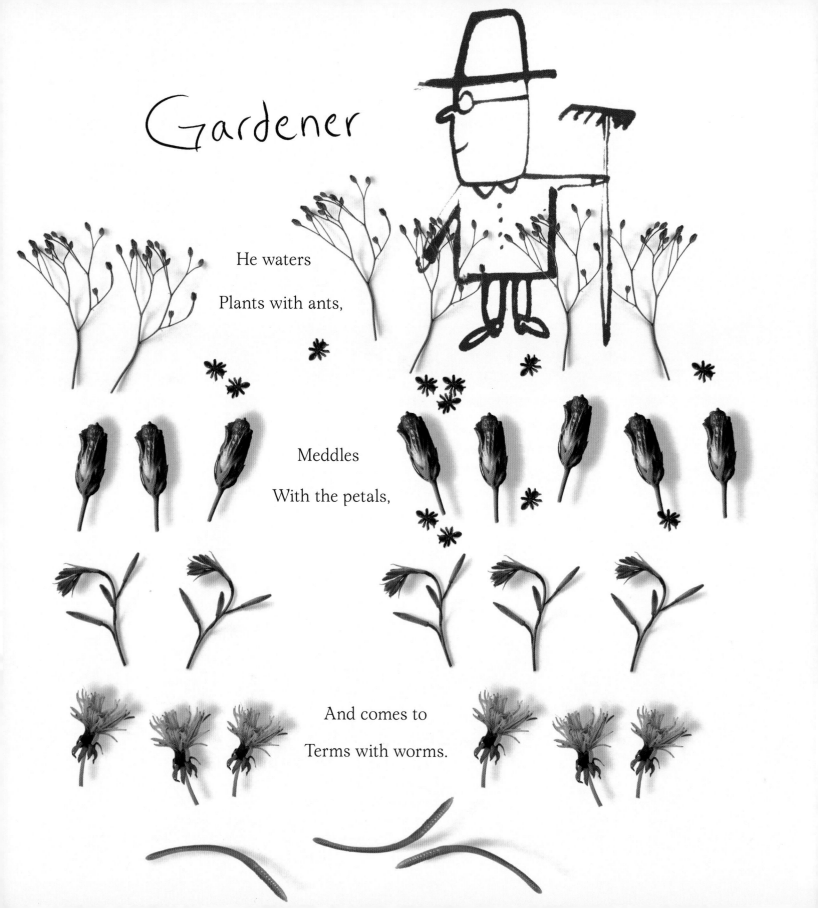

He waters
Plants with ants,

Meddles
With the petals,

And comes to
Terms with worms.

Queen of England

Royal
Goyal
Who'll
Roo'll
Isle
Awhisle

Banana Picker

Here's

my yellow

long-fellow

package

deal

that

has a

very

slippery

appeal.

Crossword Puzzle Maker

I make up clues for
"Olive" (green),

"Lentil or garbanzo" (bean).
What do "knickerbockers" mean?
(Undies!)

The Midnight Ride of Paul Re_ _ _ _?
The playwright William Shake_ _ _ _ _ _?

My best crosswords always appear . . .
(On Sundays).

Fashion Designer

Every lady in Manhattan,
I shall drape in silk and satin,
Velvet, linen, leather, suede.
I can make a bride or biddy—
Anybody!—just as pretty
As a night in New York City
Or an Easter Day parade.

Women look to me for beauty
For it is my solemn duty
To make evening gowns that fit,
To bedazzle her with riches—
Or at least keep her in stitches,
Corduroy or spandex, which is
Rather stretching things a bit.

Bridge Painter

Do not be afraid of heights
Overlooking harbor lights.
Paint the girders red and green
And cloudy colors in between.
Paint them to your heart's content;
Improvise, experiment!
With a lightning bolt or star
For the driver of the car
Gazing up at you to scan   p   a
The ultimate attention   s   n.

Then, to make the job official,
Sign the bridge with an initial.

Taxi Driver

The meter ticks,
The heater purrs,
I overhear
My passengers,

And just to show
That I can squawk,
I sing my song,
"New Yawk, New Yawk."

Bathroom Attendant

Toilet's spiffy,　　　I treat you
Sink's a shrine,　　　Like a VIP.
Mirrors sparkle,　　　You treat me
Floors all shine.　　　With a T-I-P.

614 — 5 fr.

Sword Swallower

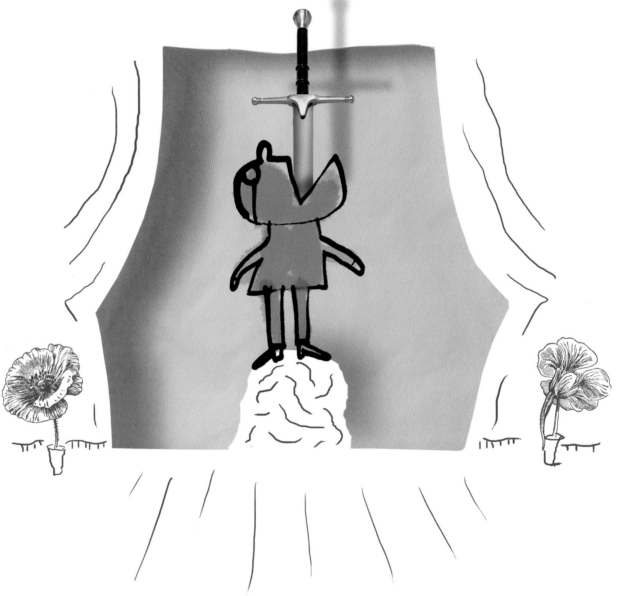

Two rules sword swallowers follow
That normally follow a swallow:

1. Look up to the ceiling.
2. Ignore your gut feeling.

Sunken Treasure Hunter

A polyp
Will crawl up
And doll up
The reef.

Sea floor'll
Be coral
Of floral—
Like leaf.

Postcard in
A garden
Boneyard in
The sea,

Whose view is
For you as
Deep blue as
Can be.

I hover
Above her,
Uncover
A ship,

Where we go,
Amigo—
This sea-
going trip—

Whose maiden
Voyage laden
Was tradin'
For gold.

Spotlight to
The right to
A sight to
Behold!

Baby Chick Inspector

Will he be a rooster?
Will she be a hen?
Delicately check the chick,
Then check the chick again.
Chickies look identical,
But you can be quite sure
If a chickie is a chickie him
Or a chickie her.

Feathers grow much faster
On a baby hen, so you
Can tell if it's a future rooster—
Cock-a-doodle-doo!

Birdwatcher

The birdwatcher keeps his long, life list,
Song notes running through it,
And feeds the feathered friends he's missed
Seed and suet.
A mockingbird relays the news
Hot off the morning wire.
A blackbird trills "Ol' Bayou Blues"—
Wings of fire.
An owl silently captures night,
Hawk steals day red-handed.
A robin turns from winter's light—
Spring has landed!

Tiger Tamer

Circus people sometimes reminisce
About tigers Miss Kitty would kiss.

Once she stuck her nose in
Where it shouldn't have been—
There's a part of Miss Kitty we miss!

Acupuncturist

I am an expert with a stick-pin that I push in.

Forgive me if I make you look like a pin-cushion!

Bicycle Champion

One hundred hours
Of fields and flowers

The endless climb
To make up time

Steep hairpin curves
Wear on your nerves

Your lungs catch fire—
A punctured tire

The legs that churn
Begin to burn

Along terrain
Mapped out by pain

A French town stops
Unloading crops

To wave adieu
Expecting you

To hit pay dirt—
The yellow shirt.

Subway Driver

B

A sixty-mile-an-hour mole
On automatic cruise control,
I worm my way around and around
Big bunny tunnels underground
With folks who stare or read or sleep
And dream of something
V E R Y D E E P.

Astronomer

I look for stars
    Too fat to hang
Far out in space
    That pop—and bang!

Their insides get
    So blazing hot—
One day they're there,
    The next they're not!

And no one knows
    Exactly why
But in the ceiling
    Of the sky,

The holes that swallow
    Starry light
Are big as day
    And black as night.

Skyscraper Window Washer

Window pain:
Ordinary words
Cannot express
My thoughts on birds.

Camp Counselor

Counselor is slated,
Campers are greeted,
Campers updated,
Campers, be seated!

Campers invaded
Counselor—short-sheeted!
Campers elated,
Counselor defeated!

Cuckoo-Clock Repairman

I am in a fix.
Don't know what to do.
Every hour, the bird pops out,
But she won't cuckoo.

I put a little oil
On the birdie's track.
Cuckoo still will not cuckoo—
Now she goes "quack-quack!"

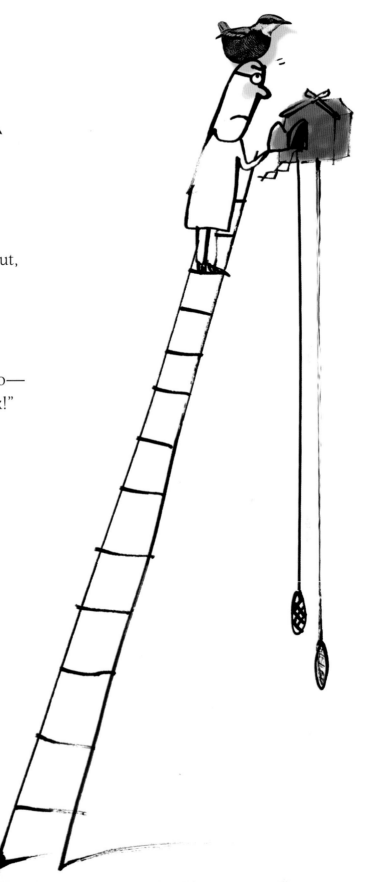

Maitre d'

Said maitre d'—
A maitre d'ude—
"Headwaiter, we
Make better food!"

What maitre d'oes
Makes waiter glad.
(The maitre d'ude's
His maitre d'ad.)

Gymnast

You want to score a perfect ten?
Then just remember how and when
To triple-handspring somersault
Or stick the landing on a vault.
A stutz? A hecht in your routine?
If you don't find out what they mean
Before you try 'em, your dismount'll
Leave you very horizontal!

Landscape Painter

What makes a field
 A field to you
Depends upon
 Your point of view.

You'd call it "MEADOW-
 LAND" unless
You were a worm—
 Then . . . "WILDERNESS."

To birds, it's "SUN-
 LIT SEA," and yet
The cow calls it
 Her "LUNCHEONETTE."

What makes a field
   A field to me
Is light—the
   possibility

That blue and yellow,
   Sun and sky
Can add, subtract, . . .
   And multiply.

All worms, birds, cows,
   And people mean
Is that a field
   Is *GREEN GREEN GREEN*.

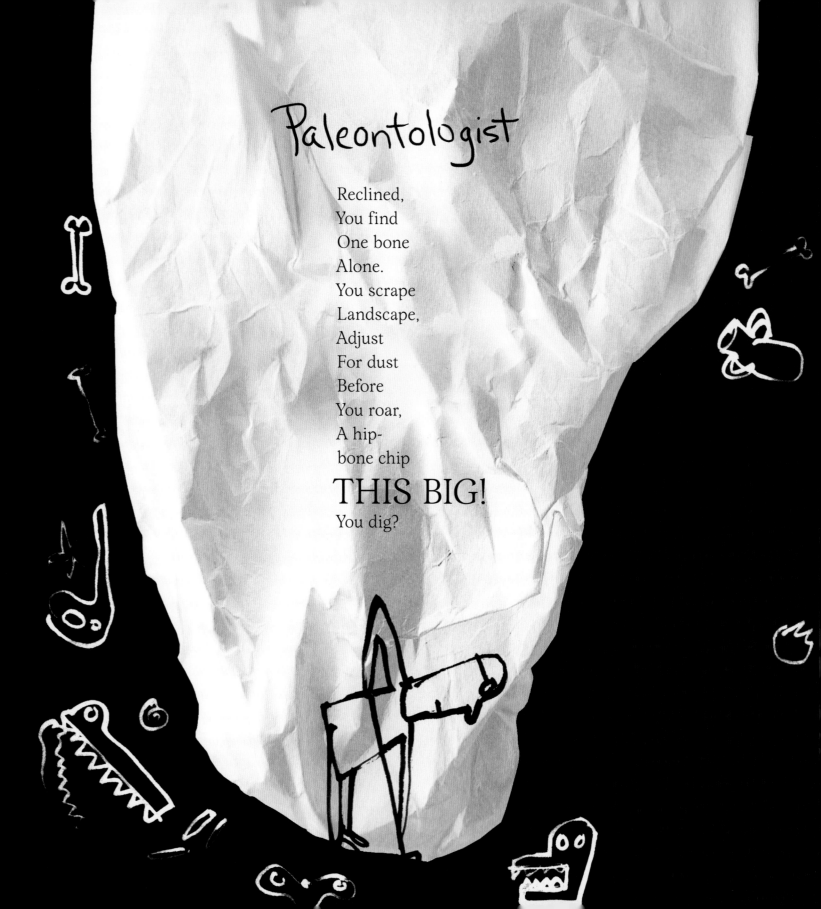

Paleontologist

Reclined,
You find
One bone
Alone.
You scrape
Landscape,
Adjust
For dust
Before
You roar,
A hip-
bone chip

THIS BIG!

You dig?

Philosopher

Self-taught,
She sought
Soft spot,
Sat squat,
Mind caught
One thought . . .
Loose knot.
Forgot.
So what?

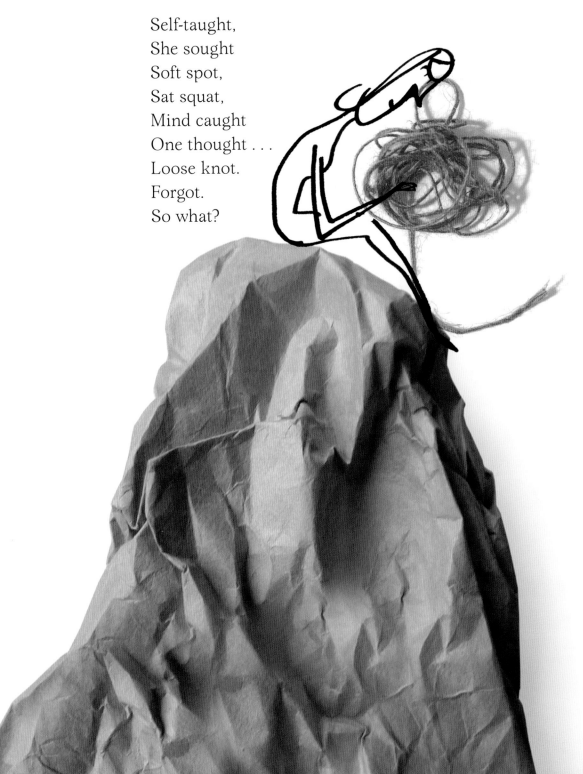

Morning Talk-Show Hosts

(**a poem** in two voices)

We play the rock 'n' roll
L.A. wakes up to,

> And talk about stuff
> People want to know,

Like whether Hubble here's
A little crazy!

> What's shakin' on your
> Morning radio?

I'm Harry, genius DJ.
Pick a topic.

> I'm Hubble, and it's *me*
> They always call

Bubble Bath Tester

Poor is poor
And rich is rich,
But in the bathtub,
Which is which?

Tennis Player

Tennis rackets all remind me,
As I hurry to the net,
Doubles matches always find me
Playing in a string quartet.

baker

deepwater diver

bouncer

A deepwater diver
Or honeybee hiver
Are fun and adventuresome,
Like oil pipe fitter,
Ninth-inning pinch hitter—
What will you decide to become?

A baker, a bouncer,
A weather announcer,
Taste tester of pink lemonade,
A dill pickle packer,
A middle linebacker,
Emcee of the Rose Bowl Parade?

A doctor, a waiter,
A crane operator,
Celebrity talent scout?
Hey, kid, what's the worry?
There's no need to hurry.
You've got your whole life to find out!

waiter

doctor

Ninth-inning

Taste tester of
pink lemonade

honeybee hiver

Emcee

dill pickle packer

crane operator

middle linebacker

weather announcer

pinch hitter